AMERICAN
BORN
CHINESE

American Born Chinese

Gene Luen Yang

Color by Lark Pien

To Ma,
for her stories of the Monkey King

And Ba,
for his stories of Ah-Tong, the Taiwanese village boy

Polytheistic

panel

THEIR MUSIC AND THE SCENT OF THEIR WINE DRIFTED DOWN . . .
. . . DOWN . . .
. . . DOWN . . .
. . . TO **FLOWER-FRUIT MOUNTAIN** . . .

. . . WHERE **FLOWERS** BLOOMED YEAR-ROUND . . .

. . . AND **FRUITS** HUNG HEAVY WITH NECTAR . . .

. . . AND **MONKEYS** FROLICKED UNDER THE WATCHFUL EYE OF THE MAGICAL **MONKEY KING.**

NOW THE MONKEY KING WAS A DEITY IN HIS OWN RIGHT.

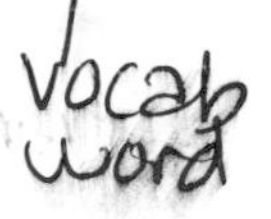
Vocab word

became king because he beat the tiger

hands/feet

THE MONKEY KING RULED WITH A FIRM BUT GENTLE HAND.
PLAY NICE.
BONK!

HE SPENT HIS DAYS STUDYING **THE ARTS OF KUNG-FU.** HE QUICKLY MASTERED THOUSANDS OF MINOR DISCIPLINES AS WELL AS THE **FOUR MAJOR HEAVENLY DISCIPLINES,** PREREQUI-SITES TO **IMMORTALITY.**

DISCIPLINE ONE: FIST-LIKE-LIGHTNING
電
KRAK!

DISCIPLINE TWO: THUNDEROUS FOOT
BOOM!
雷

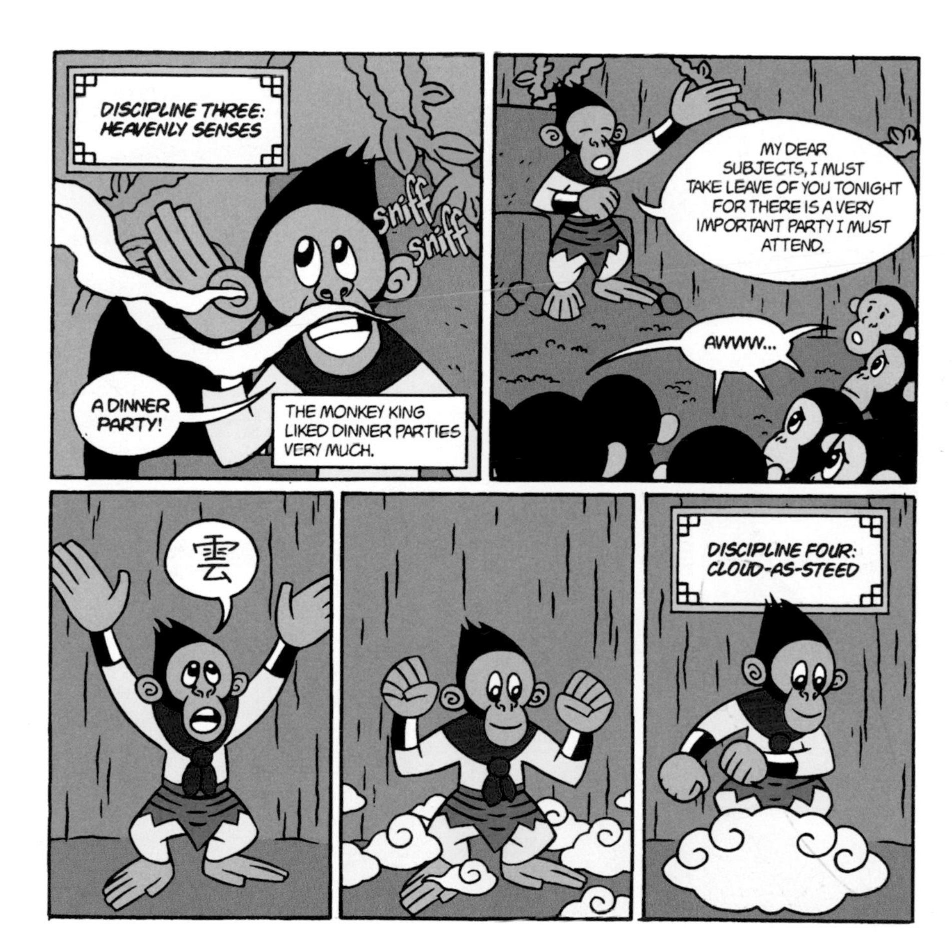
DISCIPLINE THREE: HEAVENLY SENSES
SNIFF SNIFF
A DINNER PARTY!
THE MONKEY KING LIKED DINNER PARTIES VERY MUCH.
MY DEAR SUBJECTS, I MUST TAKE LEAVE OF YOU TONIGHT FOR THERE IS A VERY IMPORTANT PARTY I MUST ATTEND.
AWWW...
雲
DISCIPLINE FOUR: CLOUD-AS-STEED

onomatopoeia/
special effects lettering

BY THE TIME THE MONKEY KING ARRIVED AT THE FRONT GATE, HE WAS BESIDE HIMSELF WITH ANTICIPATION.

ANNOUNCING THE ARRIVAL OF AO-JUN, THE DRAGON KING OF THE WESTERN SEA!

AHEM PARDON ME SIR, BUT MIGHT YOU STEP THIS WAY FOR A MOMENT?
OH, I'M SORRY-

YOU MAY ANNOUNCE THAT I AM THE MONKEY KING OF FLOWER-FRUIT MOUNTAIN!
YES, YES. I APOLOGIZE PROFUSELY SIR, BUT I CANNOT LET YOU IN-

speech balloons (external dialogue)

↑ faces ("open blank")

caption

BUT ON SECOND THOUGHT, HE DECIDED THAT PERHAPS SAYING **ONE WORD** WOULD MAKE HIM FEEL BETTER.
DIE!

gutter

bleed

KRAK!
電
電
雷
火
BOOM!

孫

background

midground

THE MONKEY KING COULDN'T STOP SHAKING AS HE DESCENDED ON **FLOWER-FRUIT MOUNTAIN.**

WHEN HE ENTERED HIS ROYAL CHAMBER, THE THICK SMELL OF **MONKEY FUR** GREETED HIM.
HE'D NEVER NOTICED IT BEFORE.

HE STAYED AWAKE FOR THE REST OF THE NIGHT THINKING OF WAYS TO GET RID OF IT.

graphic
weight

parable = a short allegorical story designed to illustrate or teach some truth, religious principle or moral lesson

< SHE FOUND A HOME ACROSS THE ROAD FROM A **UNIVERS ITY**. THE SON NOW SPENT ALL HIS FREE-TIME READING BOOKS ABOUT MATHEMATICS, SCIENCE, AND HISTORY. >

< THE MOTHER AND HER SON STAYED THERE FOR A LONG, LONG TIME. >

SHE FINISHED THE STORY AS WE PULLED UP TO OUR NEW HOUSE.

MY PARENTS ARRIVED IN AMERICA AT THE SAME AIRPORT WITHIN A WEEK OF EACH OTHER.
IRONICALLY, THEY DIDN'T MEET UNTIL A YEAR AND A HALF LATER, IN THE LIBRARY OF SAN FRANCISCO STATE UNIVERSITY. THEY WERE BOTH GRADUATE STUDENTS.
FOR TUITION MONEY, MY MOTHER WORKED AT A CANNERY.
MY FATHER SOLD WIGS DOOR-TO-DOOR.
SUAVE!
EVENTUALLY, MY FATHER BECAME AN ENGINEER AND MY MOTHER A LIBRARIAN. JUST BEFORE I WAS BORN, THEY MOVED INTO AN APARTMENT NEAR SAN FRANCISCO CHINATOWN. WE STAYED THERE FOR NINE YEARS.
楊
公司

THERE WAS A GROUP OF BOYS AROUND MY AGE THAT LIVED IN THE SAME COMPLEX.

THEY CAME OVER ON SATURDAY MORNINGS TO WATCH CARTOONS. (OUR APARTMENT, BEING ON THE TOP FLOOR, HAD THE BEST RECEPTION.)
<NO, MEGATRON!>
<DON'T DO IT!>

AFTERWARDS, WE WOULD STAGE EPIC BATTLES THAT LEFT OUR TOYS SMELLING LIKE SPIT.
PTAK! PTAK!
PTEW! PTEW! PTEW!
FFWWT!
POW!

EVERY SUNDAY MOTHER USED TO VISIT THE CHINESE HERBALIST JUST AROUND THE CORNER FOR HER ALLERGIES. SHE WOULD ALWAYS TAKE ME ALONG.
SOMETIMES THE APPOINTMENT LASTED FOR WHAT SEEMED LIKE HOURS. I WOULD SIT IN THE FRONT ROOM, LISTENING TO THE HERBALIST'S WIFE CALCULATE BILLS ON HER ABACUS.

CLICK
CLACK
CLICK

ONE SUNDAY, WHEN BUSINESS WAS ESPECIALLY SLOW AND I WAS ESPECIALLY BORED, THE HERBALIST'S WIFE ASKED,
< SO LITTLE FRIEND, WHAT DO YOU PLAN TO BECOME WHEN YOU GROW UP? >

<. . . WELL . . .>
<. . . I . . . I WANT TO BE A>
TRANS-FORMER!

. . . "TRANS-
FO-
MA?"

< YEAH! > **A ROBOT IN DISGUISE!** < LIKE THIS ONE! >

< HE CHANGES INTO A TRUCK . . . >
CLICK
CLICK
CLACK

< . . . SEE? > **MORE THAN MEETS THE EYE!**

< IN THE CARTOON, HE'S ALSO GOT A TRAILER THAT MAGICALLY APPEARS WHENEVER HE TRANSFORMS, BUT ON THE TOY IT'S A SEPARATE PIECE. >
< SO YOU WANT TO BE A . . . A . . . > "TRANS-FO-MA," < HUH? >

< YEAH . . . BUT MA-MA SAYS THAT'S SILLY. LITTLE BOYS DON'T GROW UP TO BE > TRANSFORMERS.

< OH, I WOULDN'T BE SO SURE ABOUT THAT. I'M GOING TO LET YOU IN ON A **SECRET**, LITTLE FRIEND: >

謹

<IT'S EASY TO BECOME ANYTHING YOU WISH . . .>
<. . . SO LONG AS YOU'RE WILLING TO *FORFEIT* *YOUR* *SOUL.*>

CLICK
CLACK
CLICK
CLACK

ON THE MORNING AFTER WE ARRIVED, WITH THE SCENT OF OUR OLD HOME STILL LINGERING IN MY CLOTHES, I WAS SENT OFF TO MRS. GREEDER'S THIRD GRADE AT MAYFLOWER ELEMENTARY SCHOOL.
Ww Xx Yy Zz
CLASS, I'D LIKE US ALL TO GIVE A WARM MAYFLOWER ELEMENTARY WELCOME TO YOUR NEW FRIEND AND CLASSMATE JING JANG!
JIN WANG.
JIN WANG!
HE AND HIS FAMILY RECENTLY MOVED TO OUR NEIGHBORHOOD ALL THE WAY FROM CHINA!
SAN FRAN-CISCO.
SAN FRAN-CISCO!

stereotype

YES, TIMMY.

MY MOMMA SAYS CHINESE PEOPLE EAT DOGS.

NOW BE **NICE**, TIMMY!
I'M SURE JIN DOESN'T DO THAT!
IN FACT, JIN'S FAMILY PROBABLY STOPPED THAT SORT OF THING AS SOON AS THEY CAME TO THE UNITED STATES!

THE ONLY OTHER ASIAN IN MY CLASS WAS **SUZY NAKAMURA.**

WHEN THE CLASS FINALLY FIGURED OUT THAT WE WEREN'T RELATED, RUMORS BEGAN TO CIRCULATE THAT SUZY AND I WERE ARRANGED TO BE MARRIED ON HER THIRTEENTH BIRTHDAY.
WE AVOIDED EACH OTHER AS MUCH AS POSSIBLE.

WHAT THE HELL IS THAT?!
DUMPLINGS.
sniff sniff
HMPH. STAY AWAY FROM MY DOG.
HA!
HEY BE COOL, MAN.

AW, DON'T GET YER PANTIES IN A BUNCH, GREG! LITTLE PANSY-BOY.
WHAT DID YOU CALL ME?!
LITTLE PANSY BOY.
WHAT?!
...NOTHIN', NOTHIN'.
COME ON. LET'S LEAVE BUCKTOOTH ALONE SO HE CAN ENJOY LASSIE.
HA HA! "BUCK-TOOTH!"

ABOUT THREE MONTHS LATER, I MADE MY FIRST FRIEND AT MAYFLOWER ELEMENTARY: **PETER GARBINSKY.** HE WAS A FIFTH GRADER.
Benjamin
Lauren
Brian

EVERYONE CALLED HIM "PETER THE EATER."
Benjamin
Lauren
Brian

HE INTRODUCED HIMSELF TO ME DURING RECESS ONE DAY.
GIMME YER SANDWICH AND I'LL BE YOUR BEST FRIEND.

OTHERWISE I'LL KICK YOUR BUTT AND MAKE YOU EAT MY BOOGERS.

MY FRIENDSHIP WITH PETER DEVELOPED QUICKLY.
WE HAD A NUMBER OF FAVORITE GAMES-

- "KILL THE PILL" -

- "CRACK THE WHIP" -

- AND "LET'S BE JEWS." WE USUALLY HAD TO STEAL AN ITEM OR TWO FROM MRS. GARBINSKY'S DRESSER DRAWER FOR THIS GAME.
HAR! JIN, YOU'RE SUCH A FRIGGIN' RIOT!

JUST BEFORE WINTER BREAK DURING MY FIFTH GRADE YEAR (PETER WAS IN SIXTH), PETER TOLD ME HE WAS GOING TO VISIT HIS FATHER IN PENNSYLVANIA. "THE FRIGGIN' GOVERNMENT FINALLY CAME TO ITS FRIGGIN' SENSES," HE SAID.
WHEN WINTER BREAK WAS OVER, PETER NEVER CAME BACK.

TWO MONTHS LATER, WEI-CHEN ARRIVED.
CLASS, I'D LIKE US ALL TO GIVE A BIG MAYFLOWER ELEMENTARY WELCOME TO YOUR NEW FRIEND AND CLASSMATE CHEI-CHEN CHUN!
WEI-CHEN SUN.
WEI-CHEN SUN!
HE AND HIS FAMILY RECENTLY MOVED TO OUR NEIGHBORHOOD ALL THE WAY FROM CHINA!
TAI-WAN.
TAI-WAN!
SOMETHING MADE ME WANT TO BEAT HIM UP.

謹

ROBO HAPPY
< SORRY TO BOTHER YOU, BUT YOU'RE CHINESE, AREN'T YOU? >
YOU'RE IN AMERICA.
SPEAK ENGLISH.
...EH...
...YOU- YOU- CHINESE PERSON?
YES.

...EH... WE- B- BE FRIEND?
I HAVE ENOUGH FRIENDS.
ROBO HAPPY

...SORRY? REPEAT, PLEASE?
I HAVE ENOUGH FRIENDS.
ROBO HAPPY

...EH ... WHO?
THEM.

OH.
ROBO HAPPY

* SIGH. *
< WHAT IS THAT? >
< A TOY ROBOT. >
< HE CAN CHANGE INTO A ROBOT MONKEY. >
< MY FATHER GAVE IT TO ME JUST BEFORE I LEFT. AS A GOOD-BYE PRESENT. >

< CAN I SEE IT? >
< SURE. >
OVER THE NEXT FEW MONTHS, WEI-CHEN BECAME MY BEST FRIEND.

"Everyone Ruvs Chin-Kee"
CLAP CLAP CLAP CLAP CLAP CLAP CLAP CLAP CLAP

VAN DER WAALS FORCES OF ATTRACTION ARE STRONGER WHEN MORE OF **WHAT** ARE PRESENT?
MMM.
HA HA HA HA HA
DANNY, YOU'RE DROOLING.
HA HA HA HA HA
WHAT?! OH! WELL, I- THAT HAPPENS WHEN I'M REALLY CONCENTRATING ON YOUR- I MEAN- **CHEMISTRY.**
HA HA HA HA HA
WILL YOU PLEASE STOP FOOLING AROUND? IF WE DON'T GET THIS ATTRACTION STUFF DOWN BY TOMORROW-
YOU KNOW, MELANIE, SINCE WE'RE ON THE TOPIC OF ATTRACTION, I'VE BEEN MEANING TO TALK TO YOU ABOUT SOMETHING . . .

...
I'VE ACTUALLY BEEN HOPING-
DANNY!
HOLD THAT THOUGHT.
YEAH, MA?!
* SIGH. *

I HAVE SOME EXCITING NEWS! GUESS WHO'S COMING TO VISIT!

WHO?

YOUR COUSIN CHIN-KEE!

THUD.
HA HA HA HA HA
I KNEW YOU'D BE EXCITED!
YOUR FATHER WENT TO GO PICK HIM UP AT THE AIRPORT! HE SHOULD BE HERE ANY MINUTE NOW!
DANNY, WHO'S COUSIN CHIN-KEE?

Why are there "hahas" lining the bottom of the page

COUSIN DA-NEE!
HA HA HA HA HA HA HA HA HA HA HA HA HA HA HA HA
RONG TIME NO SEE! CHIN-KEE HAPPY AS GINGER ROOT PRANTED IN NUTRITIOUS MANURE OF WELL-BRED OX!
...
HI CHIN-KEE.
HA HA HA HA HA HA HA HA HA HA HA HA HA HA HA HA

WHA--?! CONFUCIUS SAY, "HUBBA-HUBBA!"
HA HA HA HA HA HA HA HA
SUCH PLETTY AMELLICAN GIRL WIFF BOUNTIFUL AMELLICAN BOSOM! MUST BIND FEET AND BEAR CHIN-KEE'S CHILDREN!
HA HA HA HA HA HA HA HA HA HA HA HA HA HA HA HA

CHIN-KEE? IS THAT YOU OUT THERE?
...
OH NO! CHIN-KEE SO SOLLY, SO VELY SOLLY!
DIS PLETTY AMELLICAN GIRL WIFF BOUNTIFUL AMELLICAN BOSOM MUST BERONG TO COUSIN DA-NEE!
HA HA HA HA HA HA HA HA HA HA
PERHAPS CHIN-KEE CAN FIND PLETTY AMELLICAN GIRL FOR HISSELF WHEN HE ATTEND AMELLICAN SCHOOL TOMOLLOW WIFF COUSIN DA-NEE!
HA HA HA-HA HA
...?!
MA?!
OH, YOU TWO ARE GOING TO HAVE SO MUCH FUN TOGETHER!
HA HA HA HA HA

CLAP CLAP CLAP CLAP CLAP CLAP CLAP CLAP CLAP

THE MORNING AFTER THE DINNER PARTY THE MONKEY KING ISSUED A DECREE THROUGHOUT ALL OF FLOWER-FRUIT MOUNTAIN:
ALL MONKEYS MUST WEAR SHOES.

THE MONKEY KING ALSO ORDERED THAT HE NOT BE DISTURBED.
HE LOCKED HIMSELF DEEP DOWN IN THE INNER BOWELS OF HIS ROYAL CHAMBER, WHERE HE STUDIED KUNG- FU MORE FERVENTLY THAN EVER.

HE SPENT HIS DAYS TRAINING.

HE SPENT HIS NIGHTS MEDITATING.
HE ATE AND DRANK **NOTHING.**

AFTER FORTY DAYS, HE ACHIEVED THE FOUR MAJOR DISCIPLINES OF INVULNERABILITY.
DISCIPLINE ONE: INVULNERABILITY TO FIRE

DISCIPLINE TWO: INVULNERABILITY TO COLD

DISCIPLINE THREE: INVULNERABILITY TO DROWNING

DISCIPLINE FOUR: INVULNERABILITY TO WOUNDS

AFTER ANOTHER FORTY DAYS, HE ACHIEVED THE FOUR MAJOR DISCIPLINES OF BODILY FORM.
大
DISCIPLINE ONE: GIANT FORM
DISCIPLINE TWO: MINIATURE FORM
小
DISCIPLINE THREE: HAIR-INTO-CLONES
DISCIPLINE FOUR: SHAPE SHIFT

LOOK! OUR KING EMERGES FROM HIS ROYAL CHAMBER!
YAY! WE CAN ONCE AGAIN FROLIC UNDER HIS PROTECTION!
YOUR MAJESTY LOOKS DIFFERENT SOMEHOW . . .
SIRE, ON THE FIRST NIGHT OF YOUR SECLUSION, THE WINDS CARRIED THIS DOWN FROM HEAVEN.
. . .
NEW HAIRCUT?
Monkey King - You are hereby convicted of trespassing upon Heaven. Your sentence is death. Report immediately to the Underwater Palace of Ao-Kuang, Dragon King of the Eastern Sea, for your execution.
THIS NOTICE IS A MISTAKE.

孫

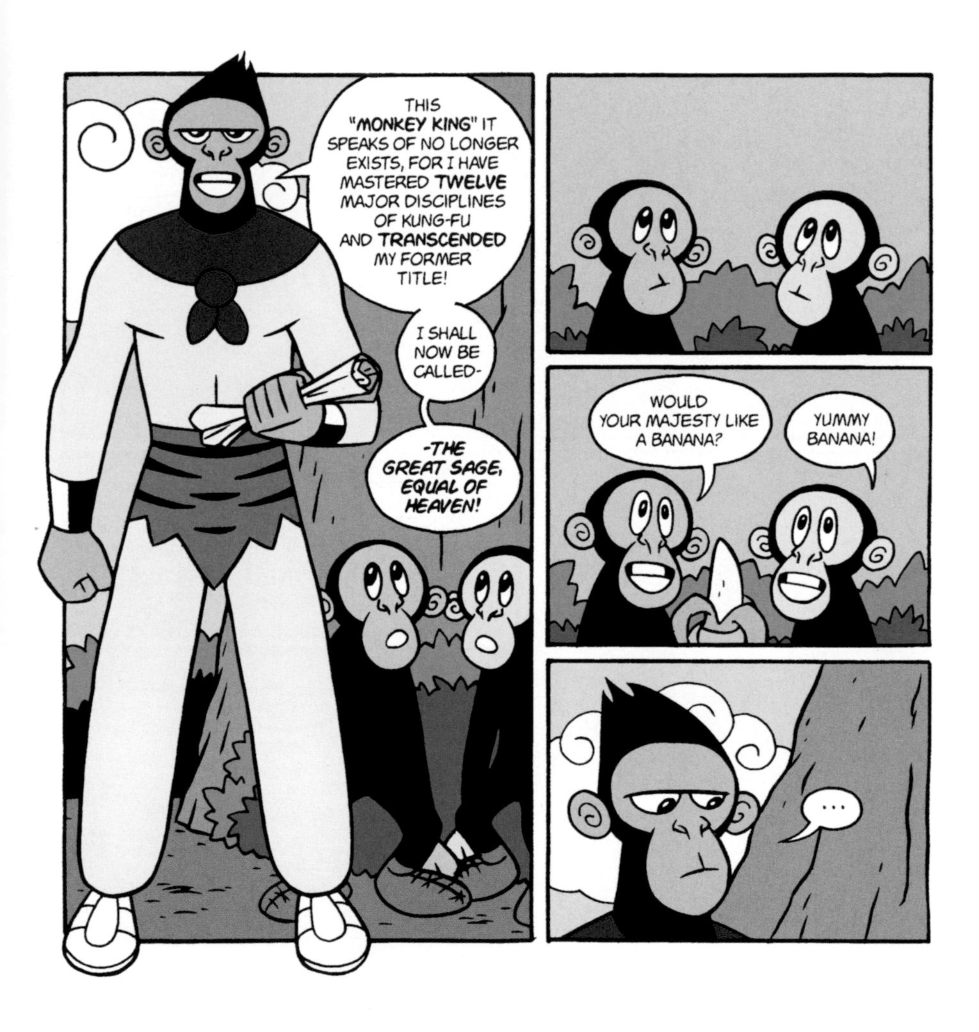
THIS "MONKEY KING" IT SPEAKS OF NO LONGER EXISTS, FOR I HAVE MASTERED TWELVE MAJOR DISCIPLINES OF KUNG-FU AND TRANSCENDED MY FORMER TITLE!
I SHALL NOW BE CALLED-
-THE GREAT SAGE, EQUAL OF HEAVEN!
WOULD YOUR MAJESTY LIKE A BANANA?
YUMMY BANANA!
...

SIRE? WHERE ARE YOU GOING?
TO ANNOUNCE MY NEW NAME TO ALL OF HEAVEN.
THOSE SHOES MUST BE WORN ON YOUR FEET, LITTLE ONE.
AWWW . . .

AO-KUANG, DRAGON KING OF THE EASTERN SEA, WAS THE FIRST TO RECEIVE THE GREAT SAGE AS A VISITOR.
AH. THE INFAMOUS MONKEY KING. I'VE BEEN ANXIOUSLY AWAITING YOUR ARRIVAL.
. . . THOUGH YOU'RE A BIT TALLER THAN I'D IMAGINED.

MY APOLOGIES FOR NOT SENDING SOMEONE TO ARREST YOU IN PERSON, BUT FRANKLY NONE OF THE GODS WANTED TO GO ANYWHERE NEAR YOUR MOUNTAIN.
NOTHING PERSONAL- WE JUST AREN'T PARTICULARLY FOND OF **FLEAS.**
NOW LET'S GET THIS OVER AND DONE WITH, SHALL WE?
GUARD!
SIR -
- THIS EXECUTION -
—plunk!
?!
- IS NO LONGER NECESSARY.
WHA - ?!
IMPRESSIVE PARLOR TRICK, LITTLE MONKEY!
I AM **NOT** A MONKEY.

HEH HEH. YOU'RE - HEH - NOT A MONKEY?
HEE HEE!
I HAVE MASTERED TWELVE DISCIPLINES OF KUNG-FU. I AM NOW THE GREAT SAGE, EQUAL OF HEAVEN.
HA HA HA!
BWA HA HA!
THE DRAGON KING NEEDED SOME CONVINCING.

THE GREAT SAGE DECIDED TO PERFORM FOR HIM THE DISCIPLINE OF GIANT FORM.
大
HA HA HA!

STOMP!
THE DRAGON KING WAS CONVINCED.

AS A PARTING GIFT, THE DRAGON KING GAVE THE GREAT SAGE A MAGIC CUDGEL THAT COULD GROW AND SHRINK WITH THE SLIGHTEST THOUGHT.

THE GREAT SAGE THEN VISITED LAO-TZU, PATRON OF IMMORTALITY . . .
HA HA HA!

. . . YAMA, CARE-TAKER OF THE UNDERWORLD . . .
TEE HEE!

. . . AND THE JADE EMPEROR, RULER OF THE CELESTIALS.
HAW HAW HAW!

ALL OF THEM NEEDED CONVINCING.

FOR LAO-TZU, THE GREAT SAGE PERFORMED THE DISCIPLINE OF **SHAPE SHIFT** . . .
!

. . . FOR YAMA, THE DISCIPLINE OF **HAIR-INTO-CLONES** . . .
!

. . . AND FOR THE JADE EMPEROR, HE DEMONSTRATED THE WONDERS OF HIS NEW **CUDGEL**.
BAP!
!

SOON AFTER, THE GODS, THE GODDESSES, THE DEMONS, AND THE SPIRITS GATHERED BEFORE THE **LION**, THE **OX**, THE **HUMAN**, AND THE **EAGLE**, EMISSARIES OF **TZE-YO-TZUH.***
PLEASE! YOU MUST ASK HIM TO DO SOMETHING!
THIS MONKEY WILL BE THE DEATH OF US!
* "HE WHO IS"
WE WILL RELAY YOUR REQUEST.

TWAK!
WHAT'S MY NAME?!
THE GREAT SAGE, EQUAL OF HEAVEN!
TWAK!
WHAT'S MY NAME?!
THE GREAT SAGE, EQUAL OF HEAVEN!
TWAK!
WHAT'S MY NAME?!
THE GREAT SAGE, EQUAL OF HEAVEN!
TWAK!

LITTLE MONKEY, WHERE DOES YOUR ANGER COME FROM?
I AM NOT-

-A MONKEY...

SILLY LITTLE MONKEY.
大
YOU WERE SAYING?
I CREATED YOU. I SAY THAT YOU ARE A MONKEY. THEREFORE, YOU ARE A MONKEY.
YOU ARE MISTAKEN. I WAS BORN OF A ROCK, CREATED BY NO ONE.

IT WAS I WHO FORMED YOU WITHIN THAT ROCK.
PROVE IT.
I AM TZE-YO-TZUH. ALL THAT I HAVE CREATED- ALL OF EXISTENCE- FOREVER REMAINS WITHIN THE REACH OF MY HAND. YOU I HAVE CREATED. THEREFORE, YOU CAN NEVER ESCAPE MY REACH.
雲
WATCH ME.

HA! TOO EASY!

!

THE GREAT SAGE FLEW WITH AS MUCH FURY AS HE COULD MUSTER.

孫

HE FLEW PAST THE PLANETS AND THE STARS.
HE FLEW PAST THE EDGES OF THE UNIVERSE.
HE FLEW THROUGH THE BOUNDARIES OF REALITY ITSELF.
* HUFF * * HUFF *

THERE, AT THE END OF ALL THAT IS, THE GREAT SAGE CAME UPON **FIVE PILLARS OF GOLD.**

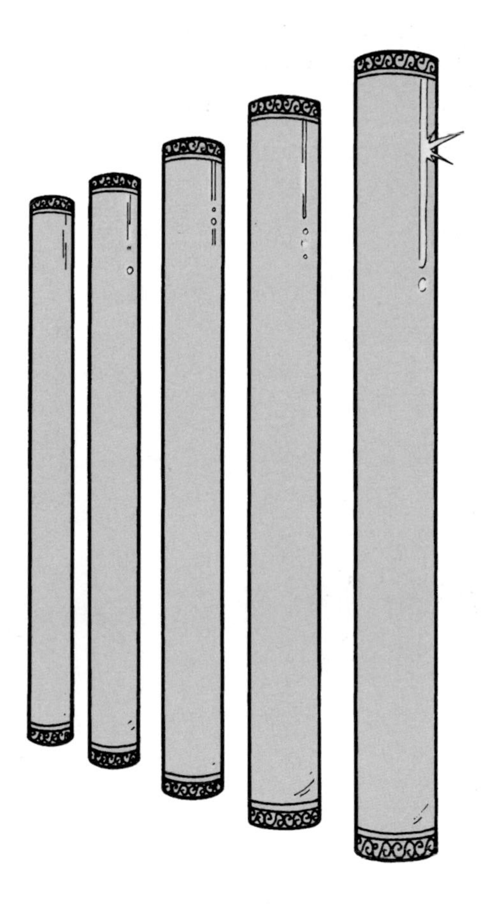

NEVER ONE TO MISS OUT ON A CHANCE FOR RECOGNITION, THE GREAT SAGE CARVED HIS NAME INTO ONE OF THE PILLARS.

THEN HE RELIEVED HIMSELF. (IT HAD BEEN AN AWFULLY LONG TRIP.)

齊天大聖到此一遊

I JUST FLEW THROUGH THE BOUNDARIES OF **REALITY ITSELF**, AND WHERE WAS YOUR "EVER-PRESENT REACH"?
NOWHERE!
HA!
OF ALL THE GODS I'VE ENCOUNTERED, YOU ARE BY FAR THE MOST **PITIABLE**.
NOW GET OUT OF MY SIGHT BEFORE I MAKE YOU RECITE MY NAME UNTIL YOUR TONGUE **BLEEDS**.
COME CLOSER, LITTLE MONKEY, AND TAKE A LOOK AT MY HAND.

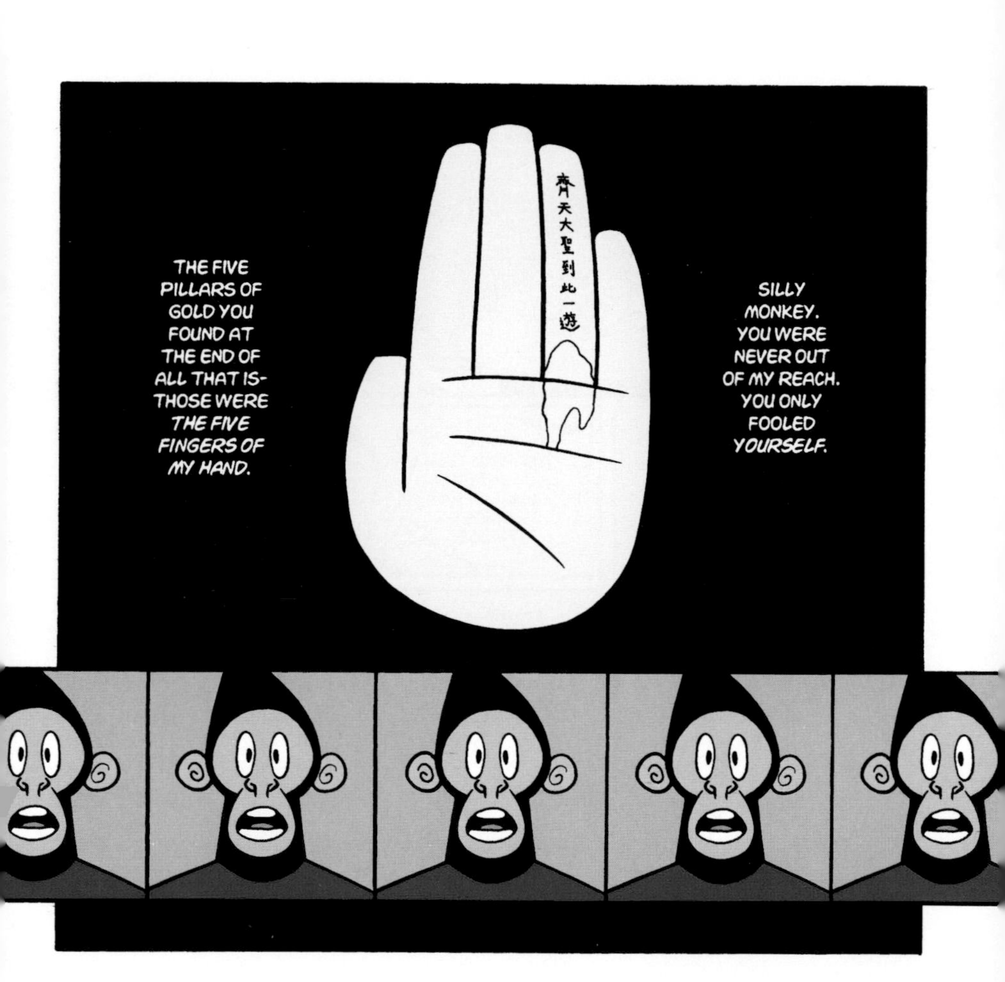
THE FIVE PILLARS OF GOLD YOU FOUND AT THE END OF ALL THAT IS- THOSE WERE *THE FIVE FINGERS OF MY HAND.*
齊天大聖到此一遊
SILLY MONKEY. YOU WERE NEVER OUT OF MY REACH. YOU ONLY FOOLED *YOURSELF.*

WALK WITH ME.
WALK WITH ME.

I AM TZE-YO-TZUH. I WAS, I AM, AND I SHALL FOR-EVER BE. I HAVE SEARCHED YOUR SOUL, LITTLE MONKEY. I KNOW YOUR MOST HIDDEN THOUGHTS. I KNOW WHEN YOU SIT AND WHEN YOU STAND, WHEN YOU JOURNEY AND WHEN YOU REST. EVEN BEFORE A WORD IS UPON YOUR TONGUE, I HAVE KNOWN IT. MY EYES HAVE SEEN ALL YOUR DAYS.
WHERE DID YOU THINK YOU COULD HIDE FROM ME? WHERE CAN YOU FLEE FROM MY PRESENCE?
I AM IN THE HEIGHTS OF HEAVEN-
-AND THE DEPTHS OF THE UNDER-WORLD.
EVEN AT THE END OF ALL THAT IS, MY HAND IS THERE, HOLDING YOU FAST.
IT WAS I WHO FORMED YOUR INMOST BEING, I WHO KNIT YOU TOGETHER IN THE WOMB OF THAT ROCK. I MADE YOU WITH AWE AND WONDER, FOR WONDERFUL ARE ALL OF MY WORKS.

I DO NOT MAKE MISTAKES, LITTLE MONKEY. A MONKEY I INTENDED YOU TO BE. A MONKEY YOU ARE.
PLEASE ACCEPT THIS AND STOP YOUR FOOLISHNESS.
I DON'T CARE WHO YOU SAY YOU ARE, OLD MAN. I CAN STILL TAKE YOU.
SIGH.

CRUMBLE

TZE-YO-TZUH BURIED THE MONKEY KING UNDER A MOUNTAIN OF ROCK AND SET A SEAL OVER HIM TO PREVENT HIM FROM EXERCISING KUNG-FU.
THE MONKEY KING STAYED THERE FOR FIVE HUNDRED YEARS.
自有者

EVEN THOUGH WE'D BEEN IN SCHOOL TOGETHER SINCE THE THIRD GRADE, I NEVER NOTICED AMELIA HARRIS UNTIL ONE HUMID AFTERNOON IN MR. KIRK'S SEVENTH GRADE ENGLISH CLASS.
zing!
LIFE WAS NEVER QUITE THE SAME AGAIN.

FROM THEN ON, SHE BECAME A TANGIBLE PRESENCE IN MY LIFE. WHENEVER SHE ENTERED THE ROOM I WAS AWARE OF HER, EVEN IF I WASN'T LOOKING DIRECTLY AT HER.
IT TOOK ME ALL NIGHT TO GET THIS STUPID THING TO W-W-W-
WOAH...
JIN? YOU OKAY?
CRASH
IT MADE ME NERVOUS THAT SOMEONE COULD HAVE SO MUCH POWER OVER ME WITHOUT EVEN KNOWING IT.

I WOULD LIE AWAKE LATE AT NIGHT ANALYZING MY FEELINGS FOR HER. SHE WASN'T EXCEPTIONALLY BEAUTIFUL AND SHE SPOKE WITH A SLIGHT LISP.
I'D EVEN SEEN A FLAKE OR TWO OF DANDRUFF WHEN I GOT CLOSE ENOUGH.

BUT WHEN SHE SMILED...
HUH HUH

I PONDERED THESE THINGS BY MYSELF FOR A FULL MONTH BEFORE TELLING WEI-CHEN.
HA HA! JIN LOVES A GIRL!

SO?
SO?! IN TAIWAN, ANY BOY WHO LOVES GIRLS BEFORE HE IS EIGHTEEN, EVERYBODY LAUGH AT HIM!
HA HA! JIN LOVES A GIRL!

THIS ISN'T TAIWAN, YOU DOOF! STOP ACTING LIKE SUCH AN F.O.B.*!
HM. THIS IS TRUE.
*FRESH OFF THE BOAT

TWO WEEKS LATER, WEI-CHEN STARTED DATING SUZY NAKAMURA.
!

謹

LOOK AT ITS EYES... SO COLD AND STILL... ALMOST LIFELESS.
I'VE NAMED HER CLARISSA, AFTER MY EX-WIFE.
HA HA

CLARISSA AND HER FRIENDS ARE ON LOAN TO US FROM BABELENE COSMETICS, INC. THIS IS A TRULY WONDERFUL AND UNEXPECTED LEARNING OPPORTUNITY FOR US, CLASS!

I HOPE YOU ALL TAKE ADVANTAGE OF IT!

MABEL, YOU REALLY MUST SAY THANK YOU AGAIN TO YOUR MOTHER.

WILL DO, MR. GRAHAM!

NOW, FOR THE DURATION OF THEIR VISIT CLARISSA AND COMPANY WILL NEED TWO STUDENT CARETAKERS. YOUR DUTIES WILL INCLUDE STAYING AFTER SCHOOL TO FEED THEM AND CHANGE THEIR WATER.
THERE WILL, OF COURSE, BE EXTRA CREDIT INVOLVED. ANY VOLUNTEERS?

THANK YOU, AMELIA.
ANYONE ELSE?
KEE
OUT

WHAT FOR, AMELIA? YOU CAN PET MY LIZARD ANY TIME YOU WANT.
TIMMY-!
KEE
OUT

I DON'T KNOW, TIMMY. YOU DO A PRETTY GOOD JOB OF THAT YOURSELF.
HA HA!
KEE
OUT

NOW IS A CHANCE FOR YOUR LIFETIME, JIN! RAISE YOUR HAND!

SHUT UP, WEI-CHEN! I AM NOT GONNA-
DON'T BE SUCH A COWARDLY TURTLE! RAISE YOUR HAND!

WEI-CHEN, ARE YOU VOLUNTEERING?

UH... IN ACTUALITY, MR. GRAHAM, JIN WOULD-
WEI-CHEN. IF YOU AREN'T VOLUNTEERING-

-THEN WHY ARE YOU MAKING SO MUCH NOISE BACK THERE?

* SIGH. *
YES, MR. GRAHAM. I WOULD LOVE VERY MUCH TO VOLUNTEER.
THANK YOU, WEI-CHEN.

KEEP OUT

YOU THINK SHE LIKES HIM?
SORRY, JIN, PLEASE SAY AGAIN? SUZY AND I WERE LOOKING AT EACH OTHER WITH EYES OF LOVE.
HA HA!
I WAS ASKING - BEFORE THE TWO OF YOU ALMOST MADE ME PUKE- DO YOU THINK AMELIA LIKES GREG?
GREG ...?
GREG, THAT GUY WHO SITS NEXT TO HER IN SCIENCE.
COME ON, JIN. DON'T BE SO PARANOID. THEY WERE JUST TALKING!
BUT TALKING IS MORE THAN HE HAS EVER DONE.
BECAUSE HE IS A LITTLE COWARDLY TURTLE.
SHUT UP. I'VE TALKED TO HER BEFORE.
YOU KNOW, I COULD BE WRONG-
-BUT I DON'T THINK DROPPING YOUR BOOKS IN FRONT OF HER AND THEN GIGGLING TO YOURSELF COUNTS AS CONVERSATION.
NO, WAIT, SUZY! WHAT HE SAY IS TRUE! REMEMBER LAST WEEK IN SCIENCE?

謹

THAT'S RIGHT! HOW COULD I FORGET?!
YES! INSTEAD OF WALKING BEHIND HER TABLE AS USUAL, JIN BRAVELY WALK RIGHT IN FRONT OF AMELIA TO GET HIS LAB MATERIALS-
-ONLY TO KNOCK OVER HALF THE TEST TUBES ALONG THE COUNTER!
AND WHEN AMELIA HELP HIM TO PICK UP THE BROKEN GLASS, JIN POINT TO TEST TUBES STILL ON THE COUNTER AND SAY-
"HUH HUH. AT LEAST I DIDN'T RAKE THE BREAST."
HA HA HA HA HA HA HA!
EVEN I DON'T MAKE SUCH A MISTAKE!

YOU-
YOU-
YOU GUYS SUCK.
HA HA HA!

HEY, I CHINK IT'S GETTING A LITTLE NIPPY OUT HERE.
YOU'RE RIGHT! I'M GETTIN' GOOK BUMPS!

HA HA HA HA HA HA HA!

...
...
...JIN?
WHAT?
WHY IS YOUR HAIR- MMPH
NOTHING! NICE PERM!
THANKS! SEE YOU GUYS AT LUNCH.
YEAH! SEE YA!
BE NICE! HE'S YOUR BEST FRIEND!
WHY IS HIS HAIR A BROCCOLI?!

謹

OOK OOK EEK!
SHE SEEMS AWFULLY ATTACHED TO YOU.

IN ACTUALITY, IT IS A **HE**.
HOW DO YOU KNOW?
ON SECOND THOUGHT, I DON'T REALLY WANT TO KNOW THE ANSWER TO THAT.

SO THIS THING EATS PINKY MICE, HUH?
THAT IS WHAT MR. GRAHAM SAY.

I THINK THEY'RE IN THE BACK CLOSET. WOULD YOU MIND GETTING THEM?
SURE.
I'M REALLY GLAD YOU'RE HERE WITH ME, WEI-CHEN. THERE'S JUST **NO WAY** I COULD DO THIS BY MYSELF. SOMETHING ABOUT LITTLE, PINK, FURLESS MICE . . .
EECH.
I WOULDN'T BE ABLE TO DEAL.

WHERE ARE THE PINKY MICE?
THEY SHOULD BE IN THERE. DID YOU CHECK BEHIND THAT BIG BOX OF BUNSEN BURNERS?
KEEP OUT
YES, I LOOK ALREADY.
HOW ABOUT BEHIND THE DOOR?
KEEP OUT
SEE? HERE THEY ARE.
KEEP OUT
CLICK
UH, WEI-CHEN?
YES?
HOW COME THERE'S NO DOOR KNOB ON THIS SIDE OF THE DOOR?
KEEP OUT

SIGH.

I CAN'T BELIEVE HOW **LAME** THIS IS. ISN'T IT ILLEGAL OR SOMETHING FOR THEM TO HAVE DOORS LIKE THAT ON CAMPUS?
DON'T WORRY!

I WAS SUPPOSED TO MEET A FRIEND OF MINE JIN AFTER SCHOOL. HE CAN FIGURE OUT WE ARE HERE.
JIN? THAT ASIAN BOY WITH THE AFRO?
YES, YES- HIM.

YOU'RE PRETTY GOOD FRIENDS WITH HIM, AREN'T YOU?
YES. JIN IS MY VERY **BEST** FRIEND. I OWE JIN VERY MUCH.
WHAT DO YOU MEAN?

WHEN I MOVE HERE TO AMERICA, I WAS AFRAID NOBODY WANTS TO BE MY FRIEND. I COME FROM A DIFFERENT PLACE. MUCH, MUCH DIFFERENT.
BUT MY FIRST DAY IN SCHOOL HERE I MEET JIN. FROM THEN I KNOW EVERY-THING'S OKAY. HE TREAT ME LIKE A LITTLE BROTHER, SHOW ME HOW THINGS WORK IN AMERICA. HE HELP WITH MY ENGLISH. HE TEACH ME HIP ENGLISH PHRASE LIKE "DON'T HAVE A COW, MAN" AND "WORD OF YOUR-" NO, NO . . .
"WORD TO YOUR MOTHER." HA HA. HE TAKE ME TO McDONALD'S AND BUY ME FRENCH FRIES. I THINK SOMETIMES MY ACCENT EMBARRASS HIM, BUT JIN STILL WILLING TO BE MY FRIEND. IN ACTUALITY, FOR A LONG, LONG TIME MY ONLY FRIEND IS HIM.

YES, I OWE JIN VERY MUCH. HE HAS A GOOD **SOUL.**
IF HE WAS NOT HERE, I DON'T KNOW. I WOULD HAVE BEEN SO **LONELY.**

CAN I ASK YOU SOMETHING, WEI-CHEN?
SHOOT AWAY.
I'VE ALWAYS GOTTEN THIS WEIRD **VIBE** FROM JIN . . .

DOES HE . . . **LIKE** ME OR SOME-THING?
HA HA! YOU YOURSELF ASK HIM!

I WAITED FOR WEI-CHEN FOR ALMOST AN HOUR BEFORE FIGURING IT OUT.
WHAT'S TAKING HIM SO LONG? HE COULDN'T'VE GONE TO MATH CIRCLES- IT'S WEDNESDAY!

IT TOOK ME ANOTHER FIFTEEN MINUTES TO CONVINCE MR. McGROUL TO OPEN THE BIOLOGY ROOM FOR ME.
NO WAY. THOSE ANIMALS IN THERE GIVE ME THE HEEBIE-JEEBIES.

I ENDED UP OWING HIM AN HOUR OF TRASH DUTY-
-AND AN ORANGE FREEZE FROM THE CAFE-TERIA.

I WAS WORRIED.
WEI-CHEN! YOU IN HERE?!
ALL ALONE WITH AMELIA?!
MAYBE A LITTLE JEALOUS, TOO.

HERE WE ARE! INSIDE THE CLOSET OF SUPPLIES!
KEEP OUT

I OPENED THE SUPPLY CLOSET AS QUICKLY AS I COULD.

EVERYTHING AFTER THAT, FOR SOME REASON, WAS A **BLUR.**

I REMEMBER THE WAY SHE LOOKED UP AT ME.

I REMEMBER WEI-CHEN WHISPERING SOMETHING IN MY EAR.
AGAIN IS A CHANCE FOR YOUR LIFETIME!

謹

I REMEMBER A JOLT OF CONFIDENCE,
ZZZT!

A STILTED QUESTION,
HANG OUT . . .
WITH ME . . .
SOME-TIME?

AND A WORD FROM HER LIPS . . .
YES.
YES.
YES.

. . . THAT KEPT ME WARM FOR THE REST OF THE NIGHT.
YES.
YES.
YES.
YES.
YES.
YES.
YES.
YES.
YES.
YES
YES
YES.

BRRRING!
OLIPHANT HIGH SCHOOL
40901
CLAP CLAP CLAP CLAP CLAP CLAP CLAP CLAP CLAP

WHY COUSIN DA-NEE BLING CHIN-KEE TO SCHOOL SO RATE? OTHER STUDENT ARLEADY IN CRASS!
JUST HURRY UP. AND STAY QUIET.
HA HA HA HA HA HA HA-HA
AH-SO! WHAT BIG, BOOTIFUL AMELLICAN SCHOOL! CHIN-KEE RIKE! CHIN-KEE RIKE VELY MUCH! HEH HEH!
HA HA-HA-HA HA HA HA HA

American Govt
COME ON, PEOPLE! LOOK ALIVE! DIDN'T ANY OF YOU DO THE ASSIGNED READING LAST NIGHT?!
LET'S TRY THIS ONE MORE TIME. THE THREE BRANCHES OF THE AMERICAN GOVERNMENT ARE . . .
OOH OOH! CHIN-KEE KNOW DIS ONE!
PUT YOUR HAND DOWN!
GO AHEAD . . . AH, CHIN-KEE, WAS IT?
HA HA HA HA HA HA HA HA
JUDICIAL, EXECUTIVE, AND REGISRATIVE!
HA HA HA HA HA HA HA HA
GOOD CHIN-KEE! VERY GOOD!
YOU KNOW, PEOPLE- IT WOULD BEHOOVE YOU ALL TO BE A LITTLE MORE LIKE CHIN-KEE.
SEE, COUSIN DA-NEE? CHIN-KEE TOL' YOU! CHIN- KEE KNOW!
HA HA HA HA-HA HA HA HA

THE NINA, THE PINTA, AND THE-
-SANTA MALIA!
HA HA HA HA HA HA HA HA
THE ULNA IS CONNECTED TO THE-
-HUMELUS!
HA HA HA HA HA HA HA HA

R² > 6R
R² > 6R
L ≤ 0
or
L ≥ 6
HA HA HA HA HA HA HA HA
EN ESTA HISTORIA, EL PERRO DE JOSÉ ES-
ESPAÑA
- BRANCO Y MUY GLANDE!
¡MUY BIEN¡
HA HA HA HA HA HA HA HA

BRRRING!
WOULD COUSIN DA-NEE RIKE TO TLY CHIN-KEE'S **CLISPY FLIED CAT GIZZARDS WIFF NOODLE?**
I'M GONNA HURL.
LEAVE ME ALONE.
HA HA HA HA HA HA HA HA
DAN THE MAN!
STEVE!

HEY, PROPS ON MAKING THE LEGENDARY OLIPHANT HIGH VARSITY BASKETBALL TEAM, KID!
COME ON, NOW. WE BOTH KNEW IT WAS INEVITABLE.
WELL, BEING AS HOW YOU'RE A TRANSFER FROM HUGHES ACADEMY, I'D SAY IT WAS ANYTHING BUT INEVITABLE. WHAT WERE YOU SCRUBS CALLED AGAIN? THE "WATER LILIES?"
OH, PLEASE. I'VE GOT A JUMP-SHOT THAT'LL MAKE YOU CRY LIKE A LITTLE SISSY GIRL.
HA HA HA HA HA HA HA HA HA
HA HA. WE'LL SEE ABOUT THAT AT PRACTICE TODAY, KID.
SO, AH . . . YOU HANGIN' WITH A NEW CROWD?
NO. THIS IS MY COUSIN CHIN-KEE.
HE'S JUST VISITING.
HARRO!
HA HA HA HA HA HA HA HA HA HA HA HA

SO HOW LONG YOU IN TOWN FOR, CHIN-K
HEY,
YOU...
YOU HAPPEN TO HAVE AN EXTRA COPY OF THE GAME SCHED-ULE?
WHY? DID YOU LOSE YOURS?
YOU KNOW, I JUST MIGHT FOR A DISORGANIZED SCRUB LIKE YOURSELF.
clink.

Cola
GIMME A SEC...
HA HA HA HA HA HA HA HA

IT'S IN HERE SOME-WHERE...

AH! IT'S YOUR LUCKY DAY, KID!
snatch!
THERE YOU GO. THAT'LL BE $100, PLUS A DATE WITH YOUR FLY GIRLFRIEND. OH WAIT- YOU DON'T HAVE A FLY GIRLFRIEND!
HA HA. THANKS, MAN.
HA HA HA HA
YOU GONNA BE AT PRACTICE TODAY?
HOW ELSE AM I GONNA MAKE YOU CRY LIKE A LITTLE SISSY GIRL?
HA HA HA HA
HA HA. SEE YOU THEN, KID.
ALL RIGHT.
♪
scoot!
OOPS! ALMOST FORGOT MY COKE.

HEE
HEE HEE

HA HA HA HA HA HA HA!
WHAT'S YOUR PROBLEM?!

ME CHINESE, ME PLAY JOKE! ME GO PEE-PEE IN HIS COKE!
BLARF!
WHAT THE HECK'S WRONG WITH MY COKE?!
HA HA HA HA HA HA HA HA HA HA HA HA HA

BRRRING!

$C_3H_8 + 5O_2 \rightarrow$
$3CO_2 + 4H_2O$
HA HA HA HA HA HA HA HA
O ROMEO, ROMEO!
WHERE-FORE ART DOU LOMEO?
HA HA HA HA HA HA HA HA

BRRRiNG!
DETENTION NOTICE
Tardy
[ ] Dress Code
Other:
Report to Room
after school.
AH. AS CONFUCIUS SAY, RAZY DOG MAKE FOR GOOD STEW.
PUNISH-MENT IS DESERVED. CHIN-KEE TOL' COUSIN DA-NEE NO COME TO SCHOOL RATE.
HA HA HA HA HA HA HA
HA HA! DIS DAY SO FUN, COUSIN DA-NEE! CHIN-KEE SO RUV AMELLICAN SCHOOL!
CHIN-KEE HAVE SUCH LORRICKING GOOD TIME!
HA HA HA HA HA HA HA HA
NOW CHIN-KEE GO TO RIBLALY TO FIND AMELLICAN GIRL TO BIND FEET AND BEAR CHIN-KEE'S CHILDREN!
PERHAPS COUSIN DA-NEE COME TOO AFTER DETENTION?
WHATEVER.
HA HA HA HA HA HA HA HA

HA HA!
HA HA HA HA HA HA HA HA
HA HA HA!
HA HA HA HA HA HA HA HA HA HA HA HA HA HA HA HA

HEY.
HEY.
LISTEN, MELANIE, I'M SOOO SORRY ABOUT ALL THAT STUFF MY COUSIN SAID-
NO. I SHOULDN'T HAVE LEFT IN A HUFF LIKE THAT LAST NIGHT. IT WASN'T YOUR FAULT.
I MEAN, IN SOME WAYS IT'S KIND OF FLATTER-ING.
HA HA HA HA HA HA HA HA

SO DOES THAT MEAN YOU'D BE UP FOR CATCHING A MOVIE WITH ME ON SATURDAY?

...
I ACTUALLY WANTED TO TALK TO YOU ABOUT THAT, DANNY. WE'RE GOOD FRIENDS, AND I REALLY **LIKE** BEING FRIENDS.

I DON'T WANT TO DO ANYTHING TO MESS THAT UP.
I'M **NOT LIKE HIM, MELANIE.**

WHAT? THIS DOESN'T HAVE ANYTHING TO DO WITH HIM!
I'M ***NOTHING*** **LIKE HIM! I DON'T EVEN KNOW HOW WE'RE *RELATED*!**

CALM DOWN, DANNY! GEEZ! THIS ISN'T ABOUT THAT, OKAY? IT'S ABOUT US BEING **FRIENDS**, AND ME NOT WANTING TO **JEOPARDIZE** THAT!

WHATEVER.

...
YOU KNOW, I NEVER NOTICED IT BEFORE, BUT YOUR TEETH KIND OF BUCK OUT A LITTLE.
HA HA HA HA HA
THEY DO?
HA HA HA HA HA
MY UNCLE'S AN ORTHODONTIST. I'VE GOT HIS CARD IN HERE SOMEWHERE.
HA HA HA HA HA
GIVE HIM A CALL. HE'LL BE ABLE TO HELP YOU OUT.
HA HA HA HA HA HA HA HA
I'LL SEE YOU AROUND, OKAY?

HATE TO TELL YOU THIS, KID, BUT PRACTICE ENDED TWENTY MINUTES AGO.
I KNOW. I HAD DETENTION.
TOO BAD. YOU MISSED THE THREE-POINTER OF THE CENTURY-
-MADE BY YOURS TRULY, OF COURSE.
HEH.
HA HA HA HA HA
YOU ALL RIGHT, DANNY?

CAN I TELL YOU SOMETHING, STEVE?
SURE, MAN. WHAT'S UP?
YOU KNOW HOW I TRANSFERRED FROM HUGHES ACADEMY AT THE BEGINNING OF THE YEAR? WELL, THE YEAR BEFORE THAT I TRANSFERRED FROM ROHMER HIGH.
I'M ONLY A JUNIOR AND I'VE ALREADY BEEN TO THREE DIFFERENT SCHOOLS.
HOW COME?
* SIGH. *
EVERY YEAR AROUND THIS TIME, I FINALLY START GETTING THE HANG OF THINGS, YOU KNOW? I'VE MADE SOME FRIENDS, GOTTEN A HANDLE ON MY SCHOOLWORK, EVEN STARTED TALKING TO SOME OF THE LADIES. I FINALLY START COMING INTO MY OWN.
THEN HE COMES ALONG FOR ONE OF HIS VISITS.
WHO?
CHIN-KEE. MY COUSIN. HE'S BEEN VISITING ME ONCE A YEAR SINCE THE EIGHTH GRADE.

HE COMES FOR A WEEK OR TWO AND FOLLOWS ME TO SCHOOL, TALKING HIS STUPID TALK AND EATING HIS STUPID FOOD.
EMBAR-RASSING THE **CRAP** OUT OF ME.

BY THE TIME HE LEAVES, NO ONE THINKS OF ME AS **DANNY** ANY-MORE. I'M **CHIN-KEE'S COUSIN.**

IT GETS SO BAD BY THE END OF THE SCHOOL YEAR THAT I HAVE TO SWITCH SCHOOLS.

COME ON, KID. IT AIN'T GONNA GO DOWN LIKE THAT HERE.
HOW DO YOU KNOW?

PEOPLE HERE AREN'T LIKE THAT. NO ONE EVER SAYS ANYTHING ABOUT MY **WEIGHT**.
WELL, MAYBE THAT'S BECAUSE I BROKE TODD SHARPNACK'S NOSE FOR CALLING ME "MR. JIGGLES" WHEN WE WERE FRESHMEN.
HA HA HA HA HA
BUT WHATEVER. PEOPLE HERE ARE DIFFERENT. YOU'LL SEE. HECK, IF ANYONE EVER GIVES YOU TROUBLE, I'LL **BREAK HIS NOSE**.
HA HA. YOU'RE PROBABLY RIGHT. THANKS, STEVE.
COME ON, KID, I'LL BUY YOU A **COKE**.
A COKE?
WHAT, SO I CAN **PEE** IN IT?
THAT'S WHAT HAPPENED TO MY COKE?
HE PEED IN IT?
HA HA HA HA HA HA HA HA

BLAAAARGFFF!
HA HA HA HA HA HA HA HA HA HA HA HA HA HA HA HA

OLIPHANT HIGH SCHOOL
40901
CLAP CLAP CLAP CLAP CLAP CLAP CLAP CLAP CLAP

IN ALL OF ANTIQUITY, ONLY FOUR MONKS EVER ACHIEVED **LEGENDARY STATUS.**

THE FIRST WAS CHI DAO, WHO FOCUSED SO SINGULARLY ON HIS MEDITATIONS THAT HIS BODY BECAME AS STONE.

THE SECOND WAS JING SZE, WHO FASTED FOR FOURTEEN MONTHS, SMIRKING IN THE FACE OF DEATH FOR THE LAST THREE.

THE THIRD WAS JIANG TAO, WHOSE SERMONS WERE OF SUCH ELOQUENCE THAT EVEN THE BAMBOO WEPT IN REPENTANCE.
I'M SO SORRY! BOO-HOO!

THE FOURTH WAS WONG LAI-TSAO, WHO WAS RATHER UNREMARKABLE BY ALL ACCOUNTS.

WONG LAI-TSAO COULD NOT MEDITATE FOR MORE THAN TWENTY MINUTES WITHOUT DEVELOPING AN ITCH IN HIS SEAT.
scratch
scratch

IF HE FASTED FOR MORE THAN HALF A DAY, HE WOULD FAINT.

WHEN HE PREACHED, HE DID NOT MAKE SENSE.
IT'S AS IF YOUR HEART HAD A DOOR ON IT. NO, WAIT- PERHAPS IT'S MORE LIKE AN EYE. NO, HOLD ON . . .
?

BUT EVERY MORNING WONG LAI-TSAO WOULD RISE WITH THE SUN . . .

. . . GATHER FRUIT IN A NEARBY ORCHARD . . .
. . . AND SHARE IT WITH THE VAGRANTS WHO LIVED JUST OUTSIDE OF TOWN.
IT'S ABOUT TIME! I'M STARVING!
IN THE AFTERNOON HE WOULD DRESS THEIR WOUNDS.
NOT SO TIGHT! WHAT'RE YOU TRYING TO DO, MAKE ME LOSE MY STUMP?!
AND IN THE EVENING HE WOULD RETURN HOME JUST AS THE SUN WAS SETTING.
TRY AND GET HERE ON TIME TOMORROW, YOU LAZY BUM!

WONG LAI-TSAO DID THIS FAITHFULLY DAY AFTER DAY, YEAR AFTER YEAR.

ONE AFTERNOON, ONE OF THE VAGRANTS ASKED,
TELL ME, MONK, WHY DO YOU COME HERE DAY AFTER DAY TO FEED US AND DRESS OUR WOUNDS?
ARE YOU TOO STUPID TO GET A REAL JOB?

I AM NO MORE WORTHY OF LOVE THAN YOU, YET TZE-YO-TZUH LOVES ME DEEPLY AND FAITHFULLY, PROVIDING FOR MY DAILY NEEDS. HOW CAN I NOT RESPOND IN KIND?

GOOD ANSWER.

AI-YA!
FLASH!

DO NOT BE AFRAID, WONG LAI-TSAO!

WE ARE EMISSARIES OF TZE-YO-TZUH, HE WHO WAS, IS, AND SHALL FOREVER BE. TZE-YO-TZUH HAS FOUND FAVOR WITH YOU.

HE HAS CHOSEN YOU FOR A MISSION.

YOU SHALL DELIVER THREE PACKAGES TO THE WEST. A STAR SHALL GUIDE YOUR WAY.

YOUR JOURNEY WILL NOT BE WITH-OUT PERIL.
IT IS AN OLD WIVES' TALE AMONG DEMONS THAT THE FLESH OF A HOLY MAN CAN GRANT ETERNAL LIFE. ONCE YOU ARE IN THE WILDERNESS, MANY WILL TRY TO EAT YOU.
DO YOU ACCEPT THIS MISSION, WONG LAI-TSAO?

I ACCEPT WHATEVER PLANS TZE-YO-TZUH HAS FOR ME.
GOOD ANSWER.
TZE-YO-TZUH HAS SEEN FIT TO PROVIDE YOU WITH THREE DISCIPLES. YOU SHALL GATHER THEM TO YOURSELF ALONG YOUR JOURNEY.
THEY SHALL ACCOMPANY YOU, PROTECT YOU, AND SHARE YOUR BURDEN.
THE FIRST OF THESE IS AN ANCIENT **MONKEY DEITY.** YOU SHALL FIND HIM IMPRISONED BENEATH A MOUNTAIN OF ROCK . . .

THE NEXT MORNING, WONG LAI-TSAO ROSE WITH THE SUN AND SET OFF ON HIS MISSION.

AFTER FORTY DAYS' JOURNEY, WONG LAI-TSAO FINALLY CAME UPON THE MOUNTAIN OF THE MONKEY KING.

?

DEAR DISCIPLE, PLEASE FREE YOURSELF QUICKLY. MY ARMS ARE THIN AND WEAK. I CANNOT BEAR THIS BURDEN ALONE MUCH LONGER.
!

WHO ARE YOU TO SPEAK TO ME IN SUCH A MANNER?! DO YOU NOT KNOW WHO I AM, MORTAL?!
YOU ARE THE MONKEY TZE-YO-TZUH PROMISED TO ME AS A DISCIPLE.
YOU FOOL! I AM THE GREAT SAGE, EQUAL OF HEAVEN!
I AM SOVEREIGN RULER OF FLOWER-FRUIT MOUNTAIN! MASTER OF TWELVE MAJOR DISCIPLINES OF KUNG-FU! COME CLOSER SO I CAN BEAT YOU FOR YOUR IMPUDENCE!
PLEASE STOP THIS NONSENSE, DEAR DISCIPLE. WE MUST BE ON OUR WAY.
ARE YOU TOO BLIND TO SEE THE MOUNTAIN OF ROCK THAT HOLDS ME TO MY PLACE, YOU IMBECILE?! EVEN IF I WERE WILLING TO SUFFER THE COMPANY OF AN IGNORAMUS SUCH AS YOURSELF, I WOULD STILL BE UNABLE TO LEAVE!

THE FORM YOU HAVE TAKEN IS NOT TRULY YOUR OWN. RETURN TO YOUR TRUE FORM AND YOU SHALL BE FREED.
IS THERE NO END TO YOUR STUPIDITY, YOU SOD?!
自有者
THAT SEAL ABOVE ME PREVENTS ME FROM EXERCISING KUNG-FU!
RETURNING TO YOUR TRUE FORM IS NOT AN EXERCISE OF KUNG-FU, BUT A RELEASE OF IT.
...

MORTAL, THERE ARE DEMONS BEHIND YOU.
YES. I AM AWARE OF THEM. THAT IS WHY I ASK YOU TO FREE YOUR-SELF QUICKLY.
AND IF I REFUSE?
IF IT IS THE WILL OF TZE-YO-TZUH FOR ME TO DIE FOR YOUR STUBBORNESS, THEN I ACCEPT.

孫

HA! THEN I SHALL ENJOY WATCHING THE DEMONS PICK YOUR FLESH FROM THEIR TEETH. IT IS A FATE BEFITTING SUCH A MORONIC TWIT.
DEAR DISCIPLE, WITH ME DIES YOUR LAST CHANCE AT FREEDOM.
"FREEDOM"?! "FREEDOM" TO SERVE AS THE SLAVE-BOY OF A MORTAL?! I'D RATHER-
STAB!

TO FIND YOUR **TRUE IDENTITY** . . .
. . . WITHIN THE **WILL** OF TZE-YO-TZUH . . .
. . . THAT IS THE **HIGHEST** OF ALL FREE-DOMS.
SO IS YOUR "TRUE IDENTITY" THE **SUPPER** OF TWO DEMONS?
PERHAPS.
. . . IS YOURS THE **ETERNAL PRISONER** . . .
. . . OF A MOUNTAIN OF ROCK?
HMPH.
!
GAAA!

SIGH.
CRUMBLE
stretch
krik
krak
dust
dust
dust
dust

WACK!
WHUMP!

合
?!

GRRRR
ROAR!
HUFF
HUFF
HUFF
swing
swing
!
ppft!

自有者
PEEYOO!
雲
自有者

KRAK
電
變

BOOOM!
大
SMACK! THUD!

LEAVE.
NOW.
ZIP! ZIP!

MORTAL-
...
MASTER. LET ME HELP YOU TO YOUR FEET.
THANK YOU...DEAR DISCIPLE.

孫

YOUR WOUNDS ARE HEAVY. I'LL FLY YOU TO THE NEAREST TOWN.
NO... NO SHORTCUTS. YOU CAN, HOWEVER... RETRIEVE THOSE... PACKAGES FOR ME.

THERE'S ONE... MORE THING, DEAR DISCIPLE.

ON THIS JOURNEY... WE HAVE NO NEED... FOR **SHOES.**

...

THE MONKEY KING ACCOMPANIED WONG LAI-TSAO ON HIS **JOURNEY TO THE WEST** AND SERVED HIM FAITHFULLY UNTIL THE VERY END.

MY MOTHER ONCE EXPLAINED TO ME WHY SHE CHOSE TO MARRY MY FATHER. "OF ALL THE Ph.D. STUDENTS AT THE UNIVERSITY, HE HAD THE THICKEST GLASSES," SHE SAID.
YOU **HAVE** TO DO THIS FOR ME, WEI-CHEN! I **HAVE** TO TELL MY PARENTS I'M WITH YOU OR THEY'RE NOT GONNA LET ME OUT AT ALL!
"THICK GLASSES MEANT LONG HOURS OF STUDYING. LONG HOURS OF STUDYING MEANT A STRONG WORK ETHIC.
IT IS LYING. I CANNOT TELL LIES.
COME ON! MY MOM PROBABLY WON'T EVEN CALL! PLUS, IT'S NOT **REALLY** LYING. I'M WITH YOU **NOW**, AREN'T I?
YOU'RE JUST TELLING A - A **DELAYED TRUTH.**
"A STRONG WORK ETHIC MEANT A HIGH SALARY. A HIGH SALARY MEANT A GOOD HUSBAND.
WEI-CHEN, I NEED YOU ON THIS ONE. OTHERWISE, IT'S NOT GONNA HAPPEN. YOU WERE THE ONE WHO TOLD ME THIS WAS "A CHANCE FOR MY LIFETIME."
PLEASE.
"YOU CONCENTRATE ON YOUR STUDIES NOW, JIN. LATER, YOU CAN HAVE ANY GIRL YOU WANT."
✳ SIGH. ✳ FINE. FOR YOU, I TELL LIES.
HA HA! I **KNEW** YOU'D COME THROUGH, MAN!
I WAS FORBIDDEN TO DATE UNTIL I HAD AT LEAST A MASTER'S DEGREE.

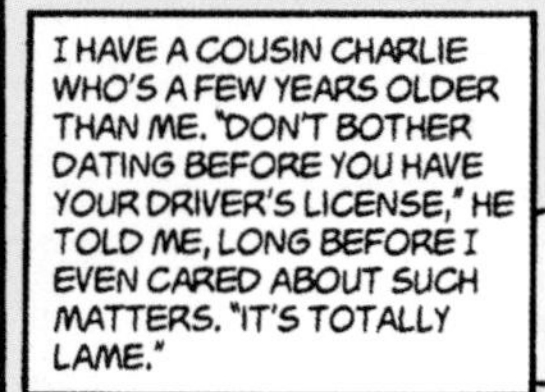
I HAVE A COUSIN CHARLIE WHO'S A FEW YEARS OLDER THAN ME. "DON'T BOTHER DATING BEFORE YOU HAVE YOUR DRIVER'S LICENSE," HE TOLD ME, LONG BEFORE I EVEN CARED ABOUT SUCH MATTERS. "IT'S TOTALLY LAME."

HUFF
HUFF HUFF

CHARLIE HAD BREATH THAT SMELLED OF OLD RICE, A BRUCE LEE HAIRCUT, AND PARENTS EVEN STRICTER THAN MY OWN, SO I ALWAYS THOUGHT IT WAS JUST SOUR GRAPES.
HUFF HUFF HUFF

NOW I'M NOT QUITE SO SURE.
HUFF HUFF

YOU OKAY?
GREAT!

HUFF

BY THE TIME WE REACHED THE THEATER, SNEAKING MY ARM AROUND HER DURING THE MOVIE WAS OUT OF THE QUESTION.
sniff
...
...
OH! IT'S ABOUT TO START!
YEAH, BECAUSE THEY- THEY JUST LURNED OFF THE TIGHTS.

I COULDN'T TELL YOU THE PLOT, ANY OF THE ACTORS' NAMES, OR EVEN THE TITLE, BUT THAT WAS THE BEST MOVIE I EVER SAW.
DURING THE FUNNY MOMENTS SHE GIGGLED IN MY EAR.
DURING THE DRAMATIC MOMENTS SHE CLUTCHED MY SHOULDER.
AND DURING THE QUIET MOMENTS I LISTENED TO HER BREATHE.

TWENTY MINUTES BEFORE CREDITS I GOT A JOLT OF CONFIDENCE.
ZZZT!

I DECIDED TO MAKE MY MOVE.
* YAWN. *

BUT I HAD TO TAKE CARE OF SOMETHING FIRST.
sniff sniff

BE RIGHT BACK.

WHEN MY PARENTS WERE GROWING UP IN CHINA, NEITHER OF THEM HAD EVER HEARD OF - LET ALONE USED - DEODORANT, SO IT NEVER OCCURRED TO THEM TO BUY SUCH A PRODUCT FOR ME.

FORTUNATELY, CHARLIE HAD SOME ADVICE ABOUT THIS PARTICULAR ISSUE, TOO.

GET SOME OF THAT POWDERED SOAP THEY GOT IN PUBLIC BATHROOMS AND RUB IT INTO YOUR PITS. WORKS THE SAME AS RIGHT GUARD.

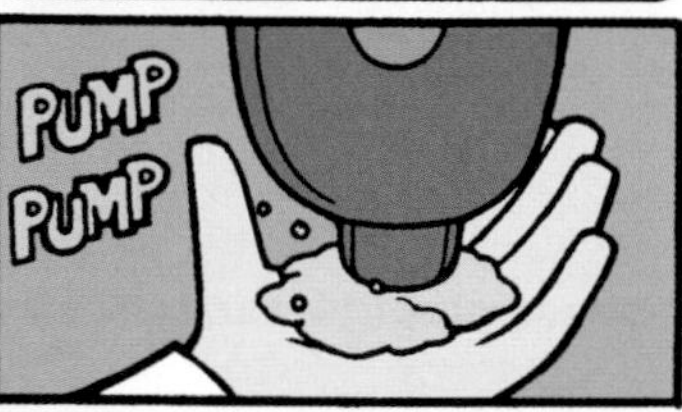
PUMP
PUMP

ZIP!
HEY.
JUST IN TIME! I THINK HE'S GONNA TELL HER HE LOVES HER...
ZZZT!
AWWW...

* YAWN. *

謹

I DIDN'T SEE IT UNTIL AFTER WE'D LEFT THE THEATER.
. . . AND WHEN HER DAD FINALLY APOLOGIZED FOR FORGETTING HER BIRTHDAY, I ALMOST CRIED.
YEAH . . . UH . . . ME TOO.
WHAT'S THAT ON HER SHOULDER?

SOAP BUBBLES?!

SO YOU WANNA GO GET MILKSHAKES OR SOMETHING?
ACK!

JIN?
MILK-SHAKES! YUM!

THERE'S THIS TLE ICE CREAM SHOP DOWN THE STREET . . .
GREAT!

THE BUBBLES HAD DISSIPATED BY THE TIME WE GOT OUR MILKSHAKES, AND AMELIA GAVE NO INDICATION THAT SHE'D EVEN NOTICED THEM.

STILL, QUESTIONS HAUNTED ME. WAS SHE JUST TOO POLITE TO SAY ANYTHING?
AND IF SO, DID SHE NOW THINK I WAS SOME SORT OF FREAK WITH BUBBLY ARMPIT SWEAT?

IN DESPERATION, I TOLD WEI-CHEN ABOUT IT THE NEXT MORNING.
AH! SHE PROBABLY DOESN'T EVEN NOTICE, JIN!
BUT TO MAKE SURE, I WILL FIND OUT FOR YOU.
WHAT?! NO! WEI-CHEN, YOU'RE JUST GONNA MAKE IT-
DON'T WORRY! I FIND OUT IN A SNEAKY WAY, LIKE NINJA. SHE WILL NOT SUSPECT. YOU WANT TO KNOW, RIGHT?
...
SEE? I FIND OUT FOR YOU.
OH! YOUR MOTHER CALL ME WHILE YOU'RE ON THE DATE. I TALK TO HER FOR TWO HOURS, TRYING FOR HER TO FORGET WHY SHE CALL.
AND . . . ?
IT WORK, BUT NOW I MUST SHOP WITH HER ON SATURDAY. SHE WILL BUY ME SHOES AND AN ELECTRIC WOK. LONG STORY.
YOU OWE ME.

HELLO AMELIA!
HEY, WEI-CHEN.
SO...
HOW WAS THE DATE WITH JIN?
...
GOOD. IT WAS GOOD.
I ACTUALLY HAD A LOT OF FUN.

FUN? HOW SO? WAS JIN NICE?
SURE.
FUNNY?
YEAH, HE-
BUBBLY?
WHAT?
DID HE . . . DID HE LOOK SOMETHING LIKE BUBBLES?
WEI-CHEN, WHAT ARE YOU TALKING ABOUT?
NOTHING!
FORGET I SAY ANYTHING! IT WAS GOOD THAT YOU HAD FUN.

FOR THE REST OF THE MORNING, I DREAMT OF OUR FUTURE.
WANNA GO OUT THIS FRIDAY?
I LOVE YOU!

I KNEW I WAS GETTING A LITTLE AHEAD OF MY-SELF, BUT I COULDN'T HELP IT. **I WAS IN LOVE.**
I'M SO HAPPY!

BE RIGHT BACK. I GOTTA GO BUY Mc GROUL AN ORANGE FREEZE.
?
!
NZZT!
HEY, JIN?

CAN I ASK YOU A FAVOR?
CAN YOU NOT ASK AMELIA OUT AGAIN?
YOU-
YOU **LIKE** HER?
WHAT?! NO, NO! SHE'S LIKE A **SISTER** TO ME! WE'VE KNOWN EACH OTHER SINCE, LIKE, PRESCHOOL OR SOMETHING. NO!
IT'S JUST THAT SHE'S A GOOD FRIEND AND I WANT TO MAKE SURE SHE MAKES GOOD CHOICES, YOU KNOW? WE'RE AL-MOST IN **HIGH SCHOOL.** SHE HAS TO START PAYING ATTENTION TO WHO SHE HANGS OUT WITH.

AW, GEEZ. LOOK, JIN. I'M SORRY. THAT SOUNDED **WAY** HARSHER THAN I MEANT IT TO. I JUST DON'T KNOW IF YOU'RE RIGHT FOR HER, OKAY? THAT'S ALL.
NO HARD FEEL-INGS?
...
YEAH.
AND YOU CAN DO ME THE **FAVOR**?
...
I GUESS.
THANKS, MAN! I APPRE-CIATE IT!

SO YOU CAN DO ME THE FAVOR?
NO.
NNZZT!
SO YOU CAN DO ME THE FAVOR?
NO!
NNKKT!
SO YOU CAN DO ME THE FAVOR?
HELL NO!
ZKRAKT!
YEAH-THE FAVOR OF A PUNCH IN THE FACE!
KRAK!

BRRING!
AMELIA!
HEY, JIN.
HOW'RE YOU DOING, JIN?

謹

...
...
SEE WHAT I MEAN? HE'S A NICE GUY, BUT HE'S KIND OF A GEEK. I MEAN, WHAT'S WITH THE HAIR?

HEY.
HEY.
WHERE'S WEI-CHEN?
MATH CIRCLES.
OH.

YOU ALL RIGHT?
I'M...
TIMMY SAID SOME-THING **STUPID** TO ME TODAY.
OH.
...
YOU KNOW, OVER THE WEEKEND I WENT TO THIS BIRTHDAY PARTY FOR LAUREN SUZUKI, MY BEST FRIEND IN SECOND GRADE.
WE USED TO GO TO JAPANESE SCHOOL TOGETHER. I HADN'T SEEN HER IN YEARS, SO WHEN MY MOM TOLD ME WE WERE GONNA GO TO HER PARTY, I WAS PRETTY **EXCITED**.

ABOUT TWENTY MINUTES INTO THE PARTY, THOUGH, I FIGURED OUT THAT LAUREN DIDN'T ACTUALLY INVITE ME. HER MOM WANTED TO HANG OUT WITH MY MOM, AND I SORT OF JUST GOT BROUGHT ALONG.
LAUREN AND HER NEW FRIENDS HAD THEIR OWN THING GOING, SO I SPENT THE REST OF THE PARTY WATCHING TV IN THE LIVING ROOM. I FELT SO **EMBARRASSED**.

...
TODAY, WHEN TIMMY CALLED ME A... A **CHINK**, I REALIZED... DEEP DOWN INSIDE... I KIND OF FEEL LIKE THAT **ALL THE TIME**.

ZZZT!

SMACK!
WHAT ARE YOU DOING?!

WHAT'S WRONG WITH YOU, JIN?!

ding dong
WHY- WHAT IS A REASON . . . WHY YOU KISS-?
< JIN, HOW COULD YOU EVEN THINK TO DO SOMETHING LIKE THIS? HOW COULD YOU HAVE EVEN LET IT ENTER YOUR MIND?! >

<IF YOU HAD FEELINGS FOR HER, YOU COULD HAVE TOLD ME. I WOULD HAVE LISTENED. I WOULDN'T HAVE TURNED MY BACK ON YOU.>

<NOW... YOU'VE BROKEN MY HEART MORE COMPLETELY THAN SUZY EVER COULD.>
<JIN... YOU AND I... WE'RE **ALIKE.**>

<WE'RE **BROTHERS,** JIN. WE'RE **BLOOD.**>

YOU HAVE **GOT** TO BE **KIDDING.**

YOU AND I ARE NOT ALIKE. WE'RE NOTHING ALIKE.

AND DON'T WORRY ABOUT YOUR STUPID GIRL-FRIEND. SHE'S NOT MY TYPE.
THEN WHY-?

MAYBE I JUST DON'T THINK YOU'RE RIGHT FOR HER, ALL RIGHT?
MAYBE I DON'T THINK YOU'RE WORTHY OF HER.
MAYBE I THINK SHE CAN DO BETTER THAN AN F.O.B. LIKE YOU.

SMACK!

I HAD TROUBLE FALLING ASLEEP THAT NIGHT. I REPLAYED THE DAY'S EVENTS OVER AND OVER AGAIN IN MY MIND.
EACH TIME I REACHED THE SAME CONCLUSION: WEI-CHEN NEEDED TO HEAR WHAT I HAD TO SAY. IT WAS, AFTER ALL, THE TRUTH.

AND AT AROUND THREE IN THE MORNING, I FINALLY BELIEVED MYSELF.

謹

I DREAMT OF THE HERBALIST'S WIFE.
CLICK
CLACK
CLICK
CLACK
CLICK
CLACK
CLICK
<SO, LITTLE FRIEND, YOU'VE DONE IT.>

<NOW WHAT WOULD YOU LIKE TO BECOME?>
CLICK
CLACK
CLICK
CLACK
CLICK

I WOKE UP WITH A START LONG BEFORE MY ALARM CLOCK WAS SUPPOSED TO SOUND.
MY HEAD HURT, BUT THE BRUISES ON MY FACE WERE GONE.

CLICK.

謹

謹

A NEW FACE DESERVED A NEW NAME.
I DECIDED TO CALL MYSELF
DANNY.
CLAP CLAP CLAP CLAP CLAP CLAP CLAP CLAP CLAP

LIBRARY
CLAP CLAP CLAP CLAP CLAP CLAP CLAP CLAP CLAP

HIS SPIT GOT ON ME!
DUDE, YOU'D BETTER GO GET CHECKED OUT FOR S.A.R.S.!
?
HA HA HA HA HA HA HA HA
TALK TO ME, TERR ME YO' NAME
YOU BROW ME OFF RIKE IT'S ALL DA SAME
YOU RIT A FUSE, I AM TICKING AWAY RIKE A BOMB
YEAH BABY!
!

SHE BANG! SHE BANG!
YEAH BABY!
SHE MOVE! SHE MOVE!
I GO CLAZY!
'CAUSE SHE ROOK RIKE FROWER BUT SHE STING RIKE BEE
RIKE EVELY GIRL IN HISTOLY!
HA HA HA HA HA HA HA HA CLAP CLAP CLAP CLAP CLAP

SHE BANG! SHE BANG!
WHA--?!
HA HA HA HA HA HA HA HA HA HA HA HA HA HA HA HA
AH-SO! HARRO! COUSIN DA-NEE FINARRY COME!
HA HA HA HA HA HA HA HA
SLAM!
RIBLALY BOLING, SO CHIN-KEE ENTERTAIN FERROW PATLONS WIFF RIVERY SONG!
COUSIN DA-NEE JUST IN TIME FOR SECOND SET!
HA HA HA HA HA HA HA HA HA HA-HA HA HA HA HA HA

I'M SICK OF YOU RUINING MY LIFE, CHIN-KEE! I WANT YOU TO PACK UP AND GO BACK TO WHERE YOU CAME FROM!

HA HA! NO NO, COUSIN DA-NEE! CHIN-KEE VISIT NOT OVER YET. CHIN-KEE NO REAVE UNTIL VISIT OVER!

GO AWAY!
CHIN-KEE STAY.

SMACK!

COUSIN DA-NEE, PREASE! NO UNDER-STAND -
HA HA HA HA HA

SMACK!

PREASE! NO MORE! COUSIN DA-NEE NOT KNOW WHAT HE IS DOING! COUSIN DA-NEE PRAY WIFF FIRE!
HA HA HA HA HA

SMACK!

AH-SO! COUSIN DA-NEE NO RISTEN, NOW MUST SUFFER UNMITIGATED FULY OF SPICY SZECHUAN DRAGON!
HA HA HA HA HA

?

WA-TA!
MONGORIAN FOOT IN FACE!
HA HA HA HA HA HA HA HA HA HA HA HA HA HA HA HA HA HA
CHIN-KEE WARN COUSIN DA-NEE! COUSIN DA-NEE NO RISTEN!
TOO BAD FOR COUSIN DA-NEE!
HA HA HA HA HA HA HA HA HA HA HA HA HA HA HA HA HA HA

AAARGH!
EEE...
THWACK!
MOOSHU FIST!
HA HA HA HA HA HA HA-HA HA HA HA HA HA HA HA HA HA HA HA HA
KUNK!
KUNG PAO ATTACK!
HA HA HA HA HA HA HA HA HA HA HA HA HA HA HA HA

TWICE COOK PALM!
CLAP!
HA HA HA HA HA HA HA HA HA
HAPPY FAMIRY HEAD BONK!
BONK!
HA HA HA HA HA HA HA HA

GENERAL TSAO ROOSTER PUNCH!
PECK PECK
HA HA HA HA HA HA HA HA HA HA HA HA HA HA HA HA HA
THUMP!
HOUSE SPECIAL KICK IN NARDS!
HA HA HA HA HA HA HA HA HA HA HA HA HA HA HA HA

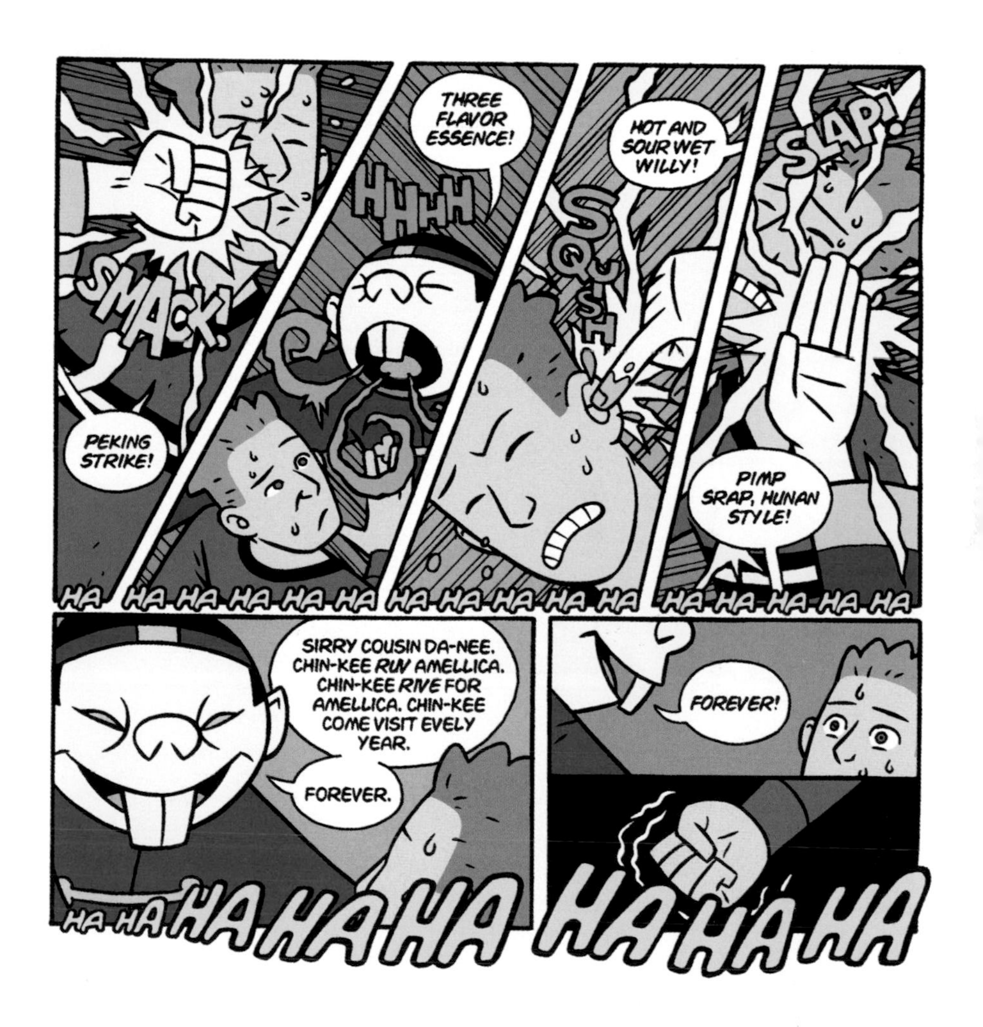
SMACK!
PEKING STRIKE!
THREE FLAVOR ESSENCE!
HHHHH
HOT AND SOUR WET WILLY!
SQUISH
SLAP!
PIMP SRAP, HUNAN STYLE!
HA HA HA HA HA HA HA HA HA HA HA HA HA HA HA HA HA HA HA
SIRRY COUSIN DA-NEE. CHIN-KEE RUV AMELLICA. CHIN-KEE RIVE FOR AMELLICA. CHIN-KEE COME VISIT EVELY YEAR.
FOREVER.
FOREVER!
HA HA HA HA HA HA HA HA HA

AAAA!
POP!
HA HA H-
bounce
bounce

鎢

NICE PUNCH.
W- W- W-
NOW THAT I'VE REVEALED MY **TRUE FORM**,
PERHAPS IT IS TIME TO REVEAL **YOURS**...

謹

Jesus

east meets west

eastern religion meets western religion

WEI-CHEN SUN, YOUR FRIEND FROM JUNIOR HIGH, IS MY SON.

WEI-CHEN?

"SHORTLY AFTER BEING INSTALLED AS EMISSARY, I HAD MY FAMILY BROUGHT TO ME."
THESE ARE ALL YOUR WIVES AND CHILDREN?!
BEING KING HAS ITS BENEFITS.

"SOON, MY ELDEST SON ASPIRED TO FOLLOW IN MY FOOTSTEPS AND BECOME AN EMISSARY HIMSELF."
THE PATH YOU ARE CHOOSING IS NOT EASY, WEI-CHEN.
I KNOW, SIR.

"FOR HIS TEST OF VIRTUE, WEI-CHEN WAS ASKED TO LIVE IN THE MORTAL WORLD FOR FORTY YEARS, ALL THE WHILE REMAINING FREE OF HUMAN VICE."
GO WITH MY BLESSING, SON. I WILL VISIT YOU ONCE A YEAR TO ASSESS YOUR PROGRESS.
TAKE THIS WITH YOU. IT'S A HUMAN CHILD'S TOY THAT TRANSFORMS FROM MONKEY TO HUMANOID FORM. LET IT REMIND YOU OF WHO YOU ARE.
GOODBYE, MY SON!
變
GOODBYE, FATHER!
YOU MET HIM DURING THE FIRST WEEK OF HIS TEST. HE SPOKE VERY HIGHLY OF YOU.
HAPPY

" WEI-CHEN'S TEST PROCEEDED WELL FOR A TIME. THEN, ON MY THIRD VISIT WITH HIM, THINGS TOOK A TURN FOR THE **WORSE.** "
I TOLD A **LIE**, FATHER.
TO THE MOTHER OF ONE OF MY CLASS-MATES.

WEI-CHEN!
YOU KNOW THE PARAMETERS OF YOUR TEST STRICTLY FORBID SUCH BEHAVIOR! WHY WOULD YOU DO SUCH A THING?!
...

...TELL ME, FATHER, WHAT EXACTLY ARE THE DUTIES OF AN EMISSARY?
EMISSARIES OF TZE-YO-TZUH **SERVE** HIM AND ALL THAT HE LOVES.

"ALL THAT HE LOVES"... THAT INCLUDES HUMANS?
YES. TZE-YO-TZUH CONSIDERS THEM THE PINNACLE OF HIS CREATION.

EVEN MORE SO THAN EMISSARIES?
YES.

TZE-YO-TZUH IS A **FOOL.** I NO LONGER WISH TO BE HIS EMISSARY.
WEI-CHEN!

I'VE FOUND HUMANS TO BE PETTY, SOULLESS CREATURES. THE THOUGHT OF SERVING THEM **SICKENS** ME.

I WILL SPEND THE REMAINDER OF MY DAYS IN THE MORTAL WORLD **USING** IT FOR MY **PLEASURE.**

WEI-CHEN, **PLEASE!** YOU MUST GIVE AN ACCOUNTING OF YOURSELF AT THE END OF YOUR TEST! HOW WILL YOU FACE TZE-YO-TZUH?!
I DON'T KNOW . . .

. . . BUT ANYTHING IS BETTER THAN A LIFETIME OF SERVITUDE TO **HUMANS.**
GOODBYE, FATHER.
WEI-CHEN!

HE REFUSED MY VISITS FROM THEN ON. I BEGAN VISITING YOU INSTEAD.

TO PUNISH ME FOR WEI-CHEN'S FAILURE.
NO, NO. WEI-CHEN'S CHOICE WAS HIS OWN. I AM NOT SO FOOLISH AS TO BELIEVE YOU HAVE POWER OVER HIS WILL.
YOU MISUNDER-STAND MY INTENTIONS, JIN. I DID NOT COME TO **PUNISH** YOU.
I CAME TO SERVE AS YOUR **CONSCIENCE** - AS A **SIGNPOST** TO YOUR **SOUL.**

雲
WAIT.

SO WHAT AM I SUPPOSED TO DO NOW?
YOU KNOW, JIN, I WOULD HAVE SAVED MYSELF FROM FIVE HUNDRED YEARS' IMPRISONMENT BENEATH A MOUNTAIN OF ROCK HAD I ONLY REALIZED HOW GOOD IT IS TO BE A MONKEY.

?
490
snatch!
490
餐 廳 餅 家
Bakery & Restau
388 9th
Oakland,
Tel: 510

HEY BA, CAN I BORROW THE CAR KEYS?
MA HAS THEM. ARE YOU TAKING CHIN-KEE OUT FOR A NIGHT ON THE TOWN?
NAH. HE WENT HOME ALREADY.
HOME?! BUT HIS FLIGHT ISN'T UNTIL NEXT WEEK!
YEAH . . . SOME-THING CAME UP. SEE YA, BA!
< HONEY, YOU'D BETTER CALL YOUR SISTER AND TELL HER TO EXPECT CHIN-KEE EARLY! >
< **MY** SISTER? I THOUGHT HE WAS **YOUR** SISTER'S SON! >

490 餐廳餅家 BAKERY CAFE

<WHAT WOULD YOU LIKE?>

OH... YEAH...
MAYBE THIS?

THAT'S NOT A DISH. THAT SAYS, "CASH ONLY."

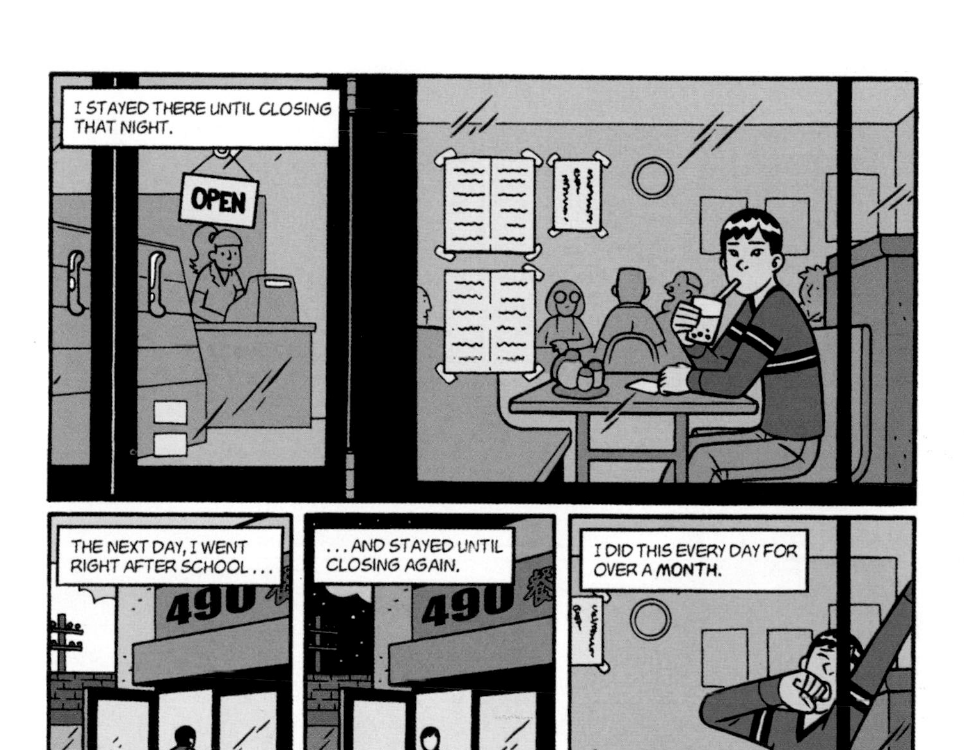
I STAYED THERE UNTIL CLOSING THAT NIGHT.
OPEN
THE NEXT DAY, I WENT RIGHT AFTER SCHOOL . . .
490
. . . AND STAYED UNTIL CLOSING AGAIN.
490
I DID THIS EVERY DAY FOR OVER A **MONTH**.

THEN FINALLY, ONE FRIDAY NIGHT, HE CAME.
PEARL MILK TEA, PLEASE.
VROOM VROOM
DA DA BUMP DA DA BUMP DA DA BUMP DA DA
BUMP DA DA BUMP
X-TREME
孫

HEY, WEI-CHEN.
JIN?!
< WHAT THE HELL DO YOU WANT?! >
I...I WANT TO TALK TO YOU.
I MET YOUR FATHER, WEI-CHEN. I JUST WANT TO TALK.

<WHY ARE YOU TELLING ME ALL THIS?>

I GUESS...

...I GUESS I'M JUST TRYING TO SAY I'M **SORRY**.
sip.

< THE MILK TEA HERE SUCKS. >
I THOUGHT IT WAS OKAY.
< THE TEA ITSELF HAS AN OILY TASTE, LIKE THEY WERE STIR-FRYING SOME-THING NEARBY WHEN THEY MADE IT. >
< THE BOBA REMINDS ME OF RABBIT CRAP. >
< THERE'S A LITTLE HOLE-IN-THE-WALL PLACE JUST DOWN THE STREET FROM HERE. BEST PEARL MILK TEA YOU'VE EVER TASTED. I'LL TAKE YOU THERE SOME-TIME. >
THAT'D BE COOL.

490 餐廳餅家 BAKERY CAFE

The End

An Imprint of Macmillan

 Printed in China by RR Donnelley Asia Printing Solutions Ltd.,
Dongguan City, Guangdong Province. For information, address
Square Fish, 175 Fifth Avenue, New York, NY 10010.

Library of Congress Cataloging-in-Publication Data

Yang, Gene.
American born Chinese / Gene Yang ; coloring by Lark Pien
p. cm.
Summary: Alternates three interrelated stories about the problems of young Chinese Americans
trying to participate in the popular culture. Presented in comic book format.
ISBN 978-0-312-38448-7
[1.Chinese Americans—Juvenile Fiction. 2. Chinese Americans—Fiction. 3. Identity—Fiction.
4. Schools—Fiction. 5. Cartoons and comics.] I. Title
PZ7.K678337 Am 2006
[Fic] dc22
2005058105

Originally published in the United States by First Second, an imprint of Roaring Brook Press
Design by Danica Novgorodoff
Chinese chops by Guo Ming Chen
Square Fish logo designed by Filomena Tuosto
First Square Fish Edition: 2009
20 19 18
macteenbooks.com
LEXILE GN530L

Thank You

Theresa Kim Yang
Kolbe Kim Yang
Jon Yang
Derek Kirk Kim
Lark Pien
Mark Siegel
Judy Hansen
Danica Novgorodoff
Thien Pham
Jesse Hamm
Jason Shiga
Jesse Reklaw
Andy Hartzell
Joey Manley
Alan Davis
Rory Root
Albert Olson Hong
Shauna Olson Hong
Hank Lee
Pin Chou
Jacon Chun
Jonathan Crawford
Jess Delegencia
Susi Jensen